0500000873181 7

D1304639

MAY 2 0 2021

Beautiful, Wonderful, Strong Little ME!

WRITTEN BY
HANNAH CARMONA DIAS

ILLUSTRATED BY
DOLLY GEORGIEVA-GODE

Eifrig Publishing LLC
Berlin   Lemont

Published by Eifrig Publishing,
PO Box 66, Lemont, PA 16851, USA
Knobelsdorffstr. 44, 14059 Berlin, Germany.

For information regarding permission, write to:
Rights and Permissions Department,
Eifrig Publishing,
PO Box 66, Lemont, PA 16851, USA.
permissions@eifrigpublishing.com, +1-888-340-6543

Library of Congress Cataloging-in-Publication Data

  Dias, Hanna Carmona
Beautiful, Wonderful, Strong Little ME! /
by Hannah Dias, illustrated by

p. cm.

Paperback: 978-1-63233-169-4
Hard cover: 978-1-63233-170-0
Ebook: 978-1-63233-171-7

[1. Self-esteem – Juvenile Fiction. 2. Diversity – Juvenile Fiction.]

I. Georgieva-Gode, Dolly, ill. II. Title

22 21 20 19 2018
5 4 3 2 1

Printed in the USA on acid-free paper with recycled content. ∞

Your Personalized Book!

CREATOR: Make your own personal audio recording of this book. Simply download the free **StorySticker** app on your Apple or Android mobile device, or visit **www.storysticker.com**. Scan the image or enter the 10-letter code to begin. Once you have set up an account and logged in, you can start to record yourself reading the story one page at a time. After you have created your own special personalized storytime, you can share it with the recipient of your book!

RECIPIENT: Just follow the instructions on the app or website to listen to the recording created just for you. Enjoy!

BRVKHFSWFD

StorySticker
all you read is love

I open my eyes and what do I see?

Beautiful, wonderful, strong little me!

With divinely dark skin that tans in the sun.
And freckles all over that dazzle and stun.

Look at my hair!
Frizzy, wild, never tame!
My gorgeous thick eyebrows
that accent my frame!

6

"I'm a smart unique girl,
happy and proud!"
I run out exclaiming
and singing out loud!

Smiling a smile that's as wide as the sky.
I see all my friends who are playing nearby.

"Lilly!" they cry out, calling my name.
I take off like lightning to join in a game.

Swinging and roaring,
Hopscotch, exploring.

Baseball and mud pies.
Clouds in the blue skies.

11

Then off to a puddle where we untie our laces;
Splash in the water and make silly faces.

In the reflection I clearly can see.
That all of my friends do not look quite like me.

"What are you?" some ask, very blunt and forthcoming,
"You look so unique that it has our mind drumming."

"Is your family Hispanic or maybe Egyptian? Indian, Brazilian, or a little Sicilian?"

"Are you white with some black? Do you come from Iraq?"

"Are you Danish or Asian?
Or mixed with some Cajun?"

17

People don't know how these questions might feel.
So I take a deep breath before my repeal.

19

"My skin and my hair
Sometimes make me stand out.
But the way that I look
Is not all I'm about."

"I'm sassy and smart
With a kind giving heart.
I'm courageous and brilliant
And fierce and resilient."

"I am not a puzzle
to figure out,

Or a mysterious artifact
to learn all about."

22

"I stand here before you
And what should you see?"

23

"A beautiful, wonderful, strong little me!"

"It's great I am different, I'm proud of my looks!
I'm not your plain princess from all of the books!"

I swish-a my hips,
And twirl-a my curl,

And show them a smile
of a confident girl.

27

I'm a beautiful, wonderful, strong little me.
And I don't need explaining to any degree!

A Note to the Reader:

The character in the book uses a variety of positive words to describe herself – words like:

Beautiful, Wonderful, Strong, Divine, Fierce, Gorgeous, Confident, Resilient, Sassy, Glamorous, Kind, Giving, Proud, Smart, and Brilliant.

What positive words can you think of to describe yourself?

Draw yourself and be sure to include all the
things that make you unique, inside and out!
(copy this page first if this is a libary book!)

About the Author

Hannah Carmona Dias is a writer who currently resides in Tennessee. **Beautiful, Wonderful, Strong Little Me** is her debut book which tackles a topic she has struggled with herself. In addition to writing, Hannah is also a wife, mother, founder of Collective Art School of Tennessee, YouTuber, and actress. When Hannah is not writing, she enjoys spending time with her family, two cats, a dog, and an iguana.

About the Illustrator

Dolly Georgieva-Gode is a freelance artist originally from Bulgaria, who lives in the United States. She works in her home studio using variety of traditional media to create vibrant images with great attention to detail. Dolly's traditional artwork has won a number of contest awards, has been published in several art books, and is currently sold in local galleries. Her hobbies are fitness, fashion and poetry. She also enjoys travel, nature and cooking healthy food. Dolly's life motto is "Be an original work of art," embracing diversity and the beauty of uniqueness.

CPSIA information can be obtained
at www.ICGtesting.com
Printed in the USA
LVHW071543130521
687354LV00013B/396